Made in the USA
Monee, IL
14 March 2023

29842076R00061